Dear Parents:

Congratulations! Your child is taking the first steps on an exciting journey. The destination? Independent reading!

STEP INTO READING® will help your child get there. The program offers five steps to reading success. Each step includes fun stories and colorful art or photographs. In addition to original fiction and books with favorite characters, there are Step into Reading Non-Fiction Readers, Phonics Readers and Boxed Sets, Sticker Readers, and Comic Readers—a complete literacy program with something to interest every child.

Learning to Read, Step by Step!

Ready to Read **Preschool–Kindergarten**
• big type and easy words • rhyme and rhythm • picture clues
For children who know the alphabet and are eager to begin reading.

Reading with Help **Preschool–Grade 1**
• basic vocabulary • short sentences • simple stories
For children who recognize familiar words and sound out new words with help.

Reading on Your Own **Grades 1–3**
• engaging characters • easy-to-follow plots • popular topics
For children who are ready to read on their own.

Reading Paragraphs **Grades 2–3**
• challenging vocabulary • short paragraphs • exciting stories
For newly independent readers who read simple sentences with confidence.

Ready for Chapters **Grades 2–4**
• chapters • longer paragraphs • full-color art
For children who want to take the plunge into chapter books but still like colorful pictures.

STEP INTO READING® is designed to give every child a successful reading experience. The grade levels are only guides; children will progress through the steps at their own speed, developing confidence in their reading.

Remember, a lifetime love of reading starts with a single step!

Materials and characters from the movie *Cars*. Copyright © 2015 Disney/Pixar.
Disney/Pixar elements © Disney/Pixar, not including underlying vehicles owned by
third parties; and, if applicable: Chevrolet is a trademark of General Motors; FIAT is a
trademark of FIAT S.p.A.; Mercury is a registered trademark of Ford Motor Company;
Porsche is a trademark of Porsche; and Volkswagen trademarks, design patents and
copyrights are used with the approval of the owner, Volkswagen AG. Background
inspired by Cadillac Ranch by Ant Farm (Lord, Michels and Marquez) © 1974. Published
in the United States by Random House Children's Books, a division of Random House
LLC, 1745 Broadway, New York, NY 10019, and in Canada by Random House of
Canada Limited, Toronto, Penguin Random House Companies, in conjunction with
Disney Enterprises, Inc.

Visit us on the Web!
StepIntoReading.com
randomhousekids.com

Educators and librarians, for a variety of teaching tools, visit us at
RHTeachersLibrarians.com

ISBN 978-0-7364-3282-5 (trade) — ISBN 978-0-7364-8218-9 (lib. bdg.)
ISBN 978-0-7364-3283-2 (ebook)

Printed in the United States of America 10 9 8 7 6 5 4 3 2 1

DISNEP · PIXAR

TO PROTECT
AND SERVE

Adapted by Frank Berrios

Illustrated by the Disney Storybook Art Team

Random House 🏠 New York

Sheriff was going
on vacation.

Two new squad cars
came to take his place.

The squad cars
were ready to keep
the town safe!
They got right to work.

The squad cars spotted
Lightning McQueen.
He was driving
too fast!

They gave Lightning
a speeding ticket.
He was not happy.

Ramone got a ticket
for driving
too low.

Guido dropped a can
on the ground.

He got a ticket
for littering!

Meanwhile, Sheriff
was enjoying
his vacation.
He was relaxing
in the hotel pool.

Suddenly, he felt
that something
was wrong.
He needed to get
back home!

Sheriff pulled up
to Radiator Springs.
He could not believe
his eyes!

The town was covered
with police tape!
What was going on?

Sheriff spotted Mater.
He was wrapped
from roof to tire
in tape!

The squad cars had
even made Lightning
go to driving school!

Sheriff tracked down
the squad cars.

They had made a
mess of the town!

Sheriff had an idea.
He knew how to make
things right!

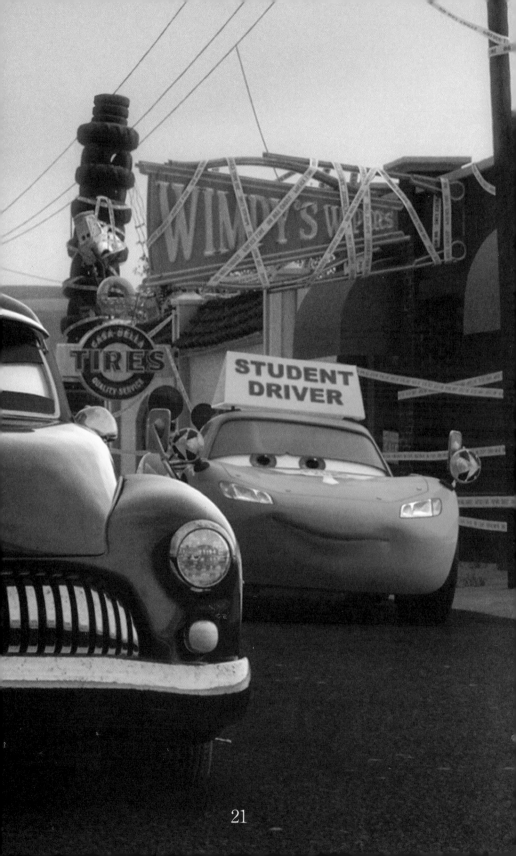

From now on,
Sheriff was going
to stay home.

The squad cars would protect him from the sun and serve him cool drinks. It was the perfect vacation!